Dot and Dan

and

Snack Attack

By Katie Dale

Illustrated by
Dean Gray

The Letter D

Trace the lower and upper case letter with a finger. Sound out the letter.

*Around,
up,
down*

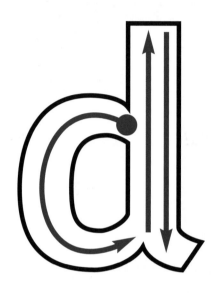

*Down,
up,
around*

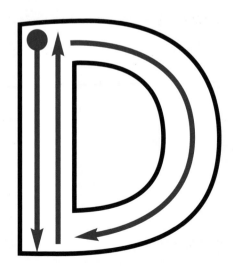

Some words to familiarise:

Dot   Dan   stuck

High-frequency words:

is not

Tips for Reading 'Dot and Dan'

- Practise the words listed above before reading the story.
- If the reader struggles with any of the other words, ask them to look for sounds they know in the word. Encourage them to sound out the words and help them read the words if necessary.
- After reading the story, ask the reader what happens when Dan eats too much.

Fun Activity

Discuss what Dan could have done to not end up being stuck.

Dot and Dan

Dan is big.

Dot is not.

Dan is full.

Dot is not.

Dan is ill.

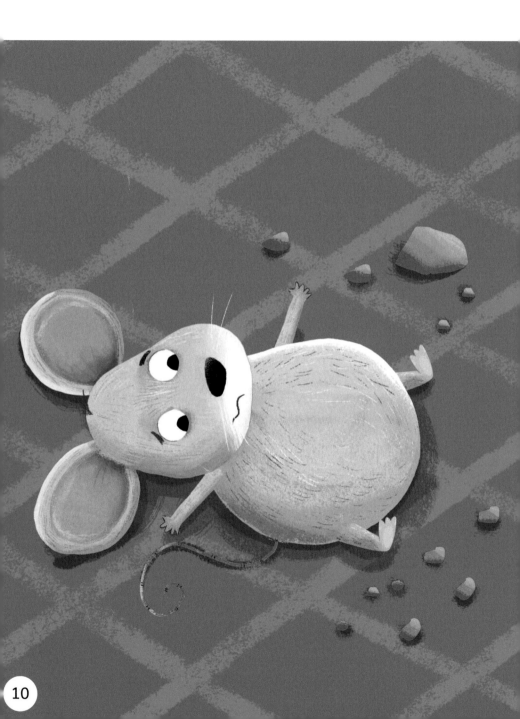

Dot is not.

Dan is fat.

Dot is not.

Dan is stuck.

Dot is not.

Dan is sad.

Dot is not.

The Letter H

Trace the lower and upper case letter with a finger. Sound out the letter.

Down,
up,
around,
down

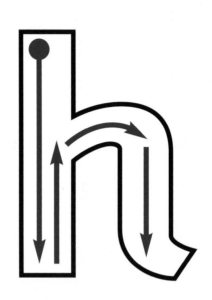

Down,
lift
down,
lift,
cross

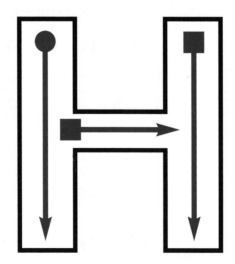

Some words to familiarise:

pot   shock   snack

High-frequency words:

a   and   the

Tips for Reading 'Snack Attack'

- Practise the words listed above before reading the story.

- If the reader struggles with any of the other words, ask them to look for sounds they know in the word. Encourage them to sound out the words and help them read the words if necessary.

- After reading the story, ask the reader how Dot and Dan get a snack.

Fun Activity

What other objects in the kitchen could you use for a tower?

Snack Attack

Dan gets a pot.

Too small.

Dot gets a mug.

Too small.

Dan gets a cup.

Too small.

Dot gets a tin.

Dan gets the snack.

CRASH!

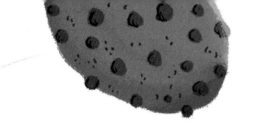

Dot and Dan get a shock!

Dot and Dan get the snack!

Book Bands for Guided Reading

The Institute of Education book banding system is a scale of colours that reflects the various levels of reading difficulty. The bands are assigned by taking into account the content, the language style, the layout and phonics. Word, phrase and sentence level work is also taken into consideration.

Maverick Early Readers are a bright, attractive range of books covering the pink to white bands. All of these books have been book banded for guided reading to the industry standard and edited by a leading educational consultant.

To view the whole Maverick Readers scheme, visit our website at

www.maverickearlyreaders.com

Or scan the QR code above to view our scheme instantly!